CW01460206

Hearts Unknown

Searching Hearts, Volume 1

Dienece Darling

Published by Dienece Darling, 2024.

HEARTS UNKNOWN

First edition. November 15, 2024.

Copyright © 2024 Dienece Darling.

ISBN: 979-8227723253

Written by Dienece Darling.

To all my supporters, thank you. I couldn't have done this without you.

Chapter One

London, 1763

I twitched my nose against the sharp scent of Father's Weymouth Pine. This was not the moment to sneeze. Not while I perched precariously in the tree behind our London terrace house.

I spared a glance at the baby bird cradled in my palm. Hopefully, its nest wasn't much farther.

I blew out a deep breath and stretched for the next branch.

"Edith Howard, you are the bane of my existence." The familiar yet unexpected voice of Clarence Beauchamp made me miss my mark.

I thrust myself forward, scrambling for a hold. The fabric of my glove ripped on the sharp scales of bark. My skin scraped across the sticky trunk, but I found no purchase. A cry tore from my throat. Not only at my own rushing descent, but that I'd lost hold of the bird. Could the tiny thing survive a second fall?

Could I?

I braced for impact. It came sooner than expected. My back thwacked into something solid, presumably my former childhood friend as he grunted and shifted.

Thick arms wrapped around me, but we were all elbows and pointy bits. Not at all romantic as I had assumed being caught by a man would be. Perhaps because it was only Clarence.

His breath skimmed my ear. "When did you get so heavy?"

The unmitigated gall.

Thankfully my feet brushed the ground, so I shoved his arms away with nary a whisper of gratitude and hurried to where the bird lay on a patch of snow, the unusual precipitation a vivid reminder of the cruel winter which had taken so much from Londoners.

"What are you doing?" Clarence chased after me.

I ignored him and plunged my hands under the delicate creature. My torn glove offered little protection from the icy pillow.

A faint chirp emitted from its strange, crisscrossed beak.

"There now, there now. Never fear, I have you. Although, I don't suppose that's reassuring after that oaf made me drop you."

"Oaf? I'm not the one who fell out of a tree." His tone bristled.

I ran a finger over the bird's ruffled feathers. "I wouldn't have fallen if you hadn't startled me."

"I saved your life."

He probably had, but no one wished to be reasonable in moments such as these.

"Pray tell..." I spun and glared at him, but the sight of a cockeyed wig atop his head smothered my fury. A laugh burst forth. "You're wearing a wig?"

Clarence straightened the white mess and squared his shoulders. "It looked perfectly respectable before you almost knocked it from my head."

"You swore you'd never fall prey to that particular 'distasteful fashion.'" I threw his own words back at him.

"We were children. We understood very little about fashion."

"I would that we were still children. You had better taste then." He'd been a more faithful friend too.

He muttered under his breath about some of us still being children, or that we were definitely not children. I paid no heed to his grumbling and stepped toward the tree.

He grabbed my elbow. "Do not resume your climb."

"Unhand me." I tugged my arm free.

"Please, listen." The gentleness of his entreaty stopped me. Clarence didn't beg.

"Why? Will you do it?" I thrust the bird at him but didn't dare peer at his face for fear of laughing at his wig again. That would ensure me no favors when I'd rather let him climb Father's pride and joy and the neighborhood menace.

What possessed Father to plant a Weymouth Pine behind our London terrace house anyway? The unsightly thing hadn't taken well to London's soil, or so Father muttered from time to time.

"You will endanger your life for naught," Clarence said.

"What do you mean?" I lifted my chin.

Shadows crowded his eyes, but he blinked them away and hardened his expression. "Put the fledgling down. It will be fine."

My jaw unhinged at such a callus remark, so unlike the boy who once rescued and raised a baby bird himself. Then mourned its loss so deeply he refused to speak of it the following winter when he came to town.

My temper surged. "You would not say the same if this were Pepin."

Clarence flinched. "The groundskeeper told me to leave him be." He stared at his feet and added in a whisper, "Would have been a kindness to us both had I listened."

I caught my breath, hoping he'd say more. I knew so little about Pepin since the rescue occurred at their country estate in the south one summer, and we were neighbors only in the city. I'd long wanted to know the story, but the haunting sadness in his eyes always kept my pressing questions in check.

"Just put it back." The sharp words couldn't hide the deep layers of pain. I knew him too well.

Part of me wanted to obey, to ease whatever ghosts still lingered in his mind, but I couldn't. The devastating winter had driven even the greedy directors of the East India Company to give ten guineas for the relief of the poor in several parishes, but the gaping needs of so many swallowed that generosity like a gnat. Such a large sum lay outside my power, and anything less seemed pointless.

All winter, my ineptitude wove around me, crushing me inch by inch until I struggled to breathe. Then I saw the bird languishing in the snow. This I could save. I needed to save it.

I dropped my gaze, unwilling to see the effect of my words on Clarence. "I can't."

Chapter Two

E dith would not look at me. After all these years, nothing had changed, not even the way I longed for her to look and really see me—not some dashing prince she'd imagined when I taught her to dance, or a duke on her generous days when she set her sights lower. But never me—boring, ordinary, follow-her-everywhere Clarence Beauchamp, second son of Baron Liffey. He was never good enough for her.

She'd never listened to me back then either.

"It won't be happy as a pet." I should know. The instant I left Pepin's cage unlatched he flew away. Much like Edith, leaving me holding a bleeding, broken heart.

'Twas my fate in life. To love where love would never be returned.

"I don't intend to make a pet of it," she said. "I want to put it back in its nest."

I studied the bird's size. "It didn't fall from the nest. It was probably learning to fly, or at least that's what the groundskeeper told me about Pepin. It's of a similar size. Put it on a branch. It will be fine."

She looked at me now, disbelief stamped on her face. "Put it on the snow encrusted branch?" She waved at the tree and descended into a passionate discourse about the bitter winter, making a particular point about spotting seagulls near London bridge. Granted, conditions had been unusually harsh, but the wild, almost desperate tint lacing her words and erratic gestures clashed with the situation. The bird was fine. It was a fledgling not a chick.

"How is a branch any different from putting it back in the nest? It's cold either way."

She blanched, a hopelessness tugging at her expression. She looked away and murmured something about never knowing what to do.

Her tear-misted eyes turned my way, and my heart lurched.

"I can't let it die, Clarence. Help me save it?"

Her pleading gaze cloyed at me, and a familiar sensation of surrender pulled me under. I never could refuse Edith, even against my better judgement. Despite the years at Cambridge, the weeks and months between terms when I repaired to the country with chums, and the last few years in town eschewing any place she might happen to be, Edith still had me under her thumb.

So much for my reputation as a bear in the courtroom.

"We should take it inside." Her face brightened. "Shouldn't we?"

No. The correct answer sat on the tip of my tongue, but some inexplicable reason drove Edith to save a bird which didn't need saving. And I couldn't disappoint her.

I heaved a sigh. "You'll need a warm box and soft rags." I scooped up the fledgling and examined it. "Nothing appears broken." Good. Much less complicated.

"That seems unlikely after two falls from a tree." Her words rang sharp with accusation.

"How was I to know you were saving a bird?"

"Why else would I be up a tree?" She regarded me oddly, as if gentlemen saw ladies in trees every day.

"How would I know? I left my parents' house after answering a summons from my father to 'visit your mother' and spotted you in a tree." Which wouldn't have happened if I'd left like a normal caller. But I'd slunk out the rear servant's entrance, hoping to escape down Bruton Mews without being spotted.

How well that worked.

"So, you do visit your parents. I wondered, since you never took a few steps to the side to visit me."

She must have missed the part about Father summoning me home. I didn't often—wait. My rambling thoughts screeched to a halt at the roaring spark in her eyes.

"Did you desire a visit?" Hope rode a cresting tide, an old, familiar, and torturous companion in my youth. Had she missed me? Perhaps wanted me as much as I wanted her?

"Did I...?" Her mouth gaped and her lashes flickered. "Of course, I did! You promised to be back for Christmas. Promised to help me with my debut but you never came. No word. No letter. Just gone. I inquired to your mother so often she became distressed at the very sight of me until I stopped asking."

The wave crashed and hope slunk back into her dark, dank corner. I was forever only Edith's friend.

And she wondered why I'd left. I ground my teeth.

We stood thus, suspended in time, until she leaned over the bird, bringing her rose scented hair near. "Will you show me how to care for it?"

I swallowed my feelings and backed away from the tantalizing fragrance. "Yes. Do you have a little box for it?"

A smile graced her lips. "I know the perfect one." She pivoted and walked toward her house.

I followed, cataloguing in my mind all the things I needed to tell her about the bird. "I should take it home with me."

"Why?" She cast a glance over her shoulder.

"The secretions for one." I transferred the bird to my other hand and wiped my soiled glove on a nearby plant.

"Oh."

"Then there are the bugs and worms they eat. Although..." I noted its distinct crisscrossed beak. "I think crossbills eat seeds." I glanced back at the Howard's pine and the copious cones dripping from its limbs. "If I may amend my statement, I'm quite certain they eat pinecone seeds, but we should mix them with bugs to be safe."

She made this adorable gagging sound.

I pressed my lips to squash a grin.

"You're enjoying this."

The heat of her glare burned, but when I turned her direction, she faced her house.

She never looked at me long enough.

—⸙—

WE'D SETTLED THE CROSSBILL in a box with soft rags when I noticed a spot of blood on one strip of fabric. I pulled the fledgling out.

"What's wrong?" Edith crowded me.

"It's hurt." I pointed at the blood.

"That isn't his." She flipped over her left hand, exposing a lacerated, blood-stained glove. I almost dropped the bird.

"What happened?" I set the creature down, my heart racing. I reached for her, but she tucked her hand behind her back. I lunged and snatched her wrist, twisting her palm up. I ripped off her torn glove.

She gasped, and I flinched, both at causing her pain and the sight of her scrapes. Her glove bore the brunt of the abuse, but any scrape was one too many on my Edith.

"Oh, some blockhead scared me while I was climbing a tree."

Horror itched down my back. "I did this?"

"Well...yes."

"Edith." Her name came out on a tortured breath. "I'm so sorry."

I tossed the glove aside and pulled her over to the pitcher and basin. I captured her gaze with mine. "This will hurt."

She gave me a brave, somewhat crooked smile and nodded.

I poured water over her injuries and reached for the soap. "Keep your hand still. This will be unpleasant, but it must be done." My heart writhed at the coming pain. Having fallen out of my fair share of trees, I knew how agonizing this part would be. Why had I startled her up a tree?

Badly done, Clarence.

I lathered the soap and touched it to her palm.

She let out a tiny groan.

I wrapped my arms around her, pulling her against my chest for support—or so I justified the move to myself. I rubbed suds around the cuts. She pressed back against me, pulling away from the pain.

I should not have enjoyed it, but she felt so good in my arms. I'd dreamed of this. Lain awake at night imagining if Edith had chosen me and not George Lucas, Esquire of Parham House. That was why I left without a word. Why I stayed away for years, hoping I'd gain control over my desires and somehow mend my hollowed-out heart. I couldn't return to playing the friend, the fool while she chased some other man.

I bit back the bitter memories and shook away the useless longings. I ignored—or at least attempted to ignore—the way she felt in my arms and poured fresh water over her cuts.

She whimpered, and the desire to kiss her temple burned so strong my mouth ran dry. I untangled my arms from around Edith and assisted her to a chair. Kneeling before her, I checked for splinters. I couldn't see any, but debris still littered her cuts. I should have washed longer. Would have too if I'd paid attention to my task and not the way she felt in my arms.

Blockhead.

I snagged my handkerchief and wet a corner of it.

The bird chirped.

"Does it need something?" Edith asked.

I inspected the creature out the corner of my eye. It seemed fine. "Baby birds just chirp. They get incessant when they want something." Memories of Pepin rushed in. He'd chirped all the time, the greedy thing. I used to wonder if I should have called Pepin, Chirp-in.

Did I truly volunteer to look after this thing for Edith?

I shook my head, flipped my handkerchief to a clean corner, and resumed my task.

"Give me leave to call on the morrow and check on the bird?" Edith asked.

"'Twouldn't be proper." I scrubbed a stubborn fleck of sap near one of her cuts.

"What's improper about calling on one's neighbors?"

"I don't live with my parents."

"Are you staying with friends?"

"No, I've taken chambers in Pall Mall East." Everything in me stilled at the unintentional admission.

"Since when?" her quiet, tentative question lashed open a jar better left shut.

The longer I'd stayed away, the more putrid that jar of questions became. Questions she had every right to demand, questions I lived in dread of answering. So, I hid, wearing wigs, doing all in my power never to face her. Pretending nothing was amiss so long as she never saw me, and no one bumped that jar.

But now it gaped open, and I had to find something to say.

"What's the meaning of this?" The sharp tone of Edith's mother filled the room.

I tensed, the situation bursting upon me how Mrs. Howard saw it—her daughter alone in a room with a gentleman at her feet holding her hand. How could I have forgotten myself? We weren't children anymore.

Edith brushed past me, her voice bright and breezy. "We rescued a baby bird, Mamma." She pointed at the crossbill.

Her mother's eyes widened. "What is that creature doing in the house?"

"It won't be here long. Clarence offered to care for it. He has lodgings on Pall Mall East. That isn't far from where we are meeting Susanne tomorrow. May we call on Clarence afterward to check on the bird?"

"Edith!" Mrs. Howard's scandalized tone cut through the room. She dropped her voice, but I still heard her next words. "Ladies may not call on gentlemen."

"Pish, 'tis only Clarence." If one ever needed proof Edith did not see me as I saw her, this was it.

In strict tones Mrs. Howard explained 'the rules very much applied,' but even so, I let myself picture it. Those three ladies in my modest sitting room. Of Edith in my home.

It would be utterly marvelous.

And completely disastrous to my heart.

Oh, I had not conquered my feelings for Edith, not even a little bit.

Chapter Three

"What do you think of this?" My sister held something white. Possibly a piece of lace, but I couldn't be bothered to focus on it.

I hummed a noncommittal reply, and Susanne appealed to Mother, a more willing participant. The sounds of the shop and busy street outside retreated once more.

When had Clarence moved to London?

With my family estate in Northumberland and his in Surrey, there was no hope of 'accidentally' meeting him in the country. Every winter when we came to town, I searched for him. Hoping for even a glimpse. He couldn't have lived here long, or I'd have seen him at his parents' dinner parties, or a ball, or the opera, or...somewhere.

"Mamma, did you know Clarence lives in town?"

"Yes, dear."

"Why did you never mention it to me?"

She drew back. "You never asked."

No, I hadn't. Not for years.

Before Clarence left for his second year at Cambridge, I'd requested his help with my debut. I trusted his judgement more than my sot of a brother. Clarence gave his solemn word to assist me, but that Christmas break had come and gone without him making an appearance.

Had he intended not to return all along?

Nay, 'twould be disloyal to think so.

Yet fear crept in, cold and unwelcome, sinking into the cracks and crevices of my aching heart with her insidious whisper. *If he had indeed been your friend.*

No, Clarence was my friend.

Then why did he stay away? Fear said.

Surely, something had delayed him, prevented him. There had to be a reasonable explanation.

"Mamma, how long has Clarence lived in London?"

"He pursued law after Cambridge, dear."

See? The cold whisper curled around me. *He's lived here for years.*

But how was that possible? "Why have I never seen him?"

"He attends his club. His mother has quite despaired of him finding a wife."

Susanne returned from making a purchase. "Of whom are we speaking?" She tucked the wrapped package under her arm, her already bulging basket unable to hold a thimble more.

"Clarence."

"What about him?" She shifted her new package a little higher.

"We were wondering why he never attends social events," I said.

"Oh, but he does."

"When? Where?" I crowded her.

"Well, he hasn't of late, but I saw him at the Melrose's rout over the summer." Susanne rattled off a few other summer events. Things she attended as she lived in town with her husband year-round.

"Oh, we were in the country." Mother nodded, satisfied.

But why attend functions out of season and eschew them when he ought to attend? Why never call on me?

Unless he meant to avoid me.

Fear gave a pernicious chuckle, and a cold band cinched my chest. Yesterday was not the first time he'd called me his bane, and it hadn't just been his mother who grew uncomfortable when I inquired after Clarence. They'd all sent me pitying looks and offered empty excuses until I stopped asking. Afraid someone would tell me one day how Clarence had rejoiced to rid himself of the pesky Howard girl.

Fear crowed her triumph, and I blinked back tears.

We left the haberdashery and walked toward our carriage. The crowds on the busy street mimicked the thoughts in my head. Swarms, converging without meaning or rhythm, and a foul odor underpinning it all.

Mother and Susanne spoke of everyday things, but I couldn't attend, couldn't enjoy the trip which normally brought me such pleasure.

I skirted a large puddle of refuse.

"The world will end on the twenty-eighth of this month!" A fellow bellowed near us. The streets of London always bustled with a cacophony of garish cries, but the vehemence in his tone took me aback.

Unfortunately, the pile of refuse lay behind.

Something squelched and slid under my foot. I scrambled for purchase for the second time in as many days, just as desperate not to take a plunge.

I lurched with flaying arms away from the muck and straight into the path of an oncoming cart.

The driver yelled and yanked on the reins. The horse screamed and reared. Hoofs clawed the air above my head.

I buckled my knees, collapsing straight down. Putting out my good hand to catch myself, I slammed into the ground. Waves of pain shot up my arm and jarred my shoulder. I curled away from the horse just in time. Its hooves clashed on the cobblestones inches from me.

"Edith." Mother's cry came a little late for all that occurred.

I tucked my new injury close and took stock of myself. My fashionable glove had proved a pitiful rival against the cobblestones. I now boasted a matching pair of scraped hands, if one could ever wish for such a set. The hem of my gown dipped into the filth, and my shoulder screamed at me.

"Edith!" An unexpected voice interrupted my inspection.

I tipped my head back, cast a look around, and spotted Clarence rushing our way.

Yes, he lived nearby, but we oft shopped here. Hitherto, we'd never crossed paths. Had I been mistaken assuming Clarence avoided me? Perhaps, I had been blind to him weaving among the masses of London.

But how could that be when I searched for him? Missed his friendship so much a gaping void occupied his place in my life.

Susanne fussed and whimpered, unsure what to do with her packages when she wanted to assist me. Mother dragged my hem from the filth, but 'twas Clarence who pulled me away from the still present danger of other carriages and horses on the road.

"Are you hurt?" he asked.

I held out my right palm, scraped and bleeding.

"Let me assist you." He scooped me into his arms without so much as a 'by your leave.'

His arms felt good, solid, safe. His chest warm.

Dazed, I studied his face, so close to mine. "You aren't wearing your wig."

His lips pressed into a line. "A girl I once knew laughed at it." The clipped words revealed so much, driving a spike deep into my heart.

"I'm sorry, Clarence." For everything, even the bits I didn't understand.

My arm throbbed, and the world rushed like a whirlpool. Mayhap I could rest on Clarence's shoulder. It looked so inviting.

Inch by inch, I dropped my head, the wool of his greatcoat somehow both rough and soft against my cheek.

His breath hitched, and his stride faltered. But he recovered and marched on as if nothing unusual occurred.

I closed my eyes and relaxed. The smell of wool mixed with something purely Clarence. It filled my senses and took me back to our dance lessons. How I missed my friend—the one I'd thought would always be there. The one I'd thought liked me. Another pang shot through my heart. I buried my face into his upturned collar and let the sobs burning my throat free.

Chapter Four

E dith stifled a whimper, but with her lips so close to my ear, I couldn't miss the sound.

Oh, my darling. I bit back the endearment until my jaw ached. "We're almost there. I promise." I pulled her closer.

My lodgings came into view, and I hurried up the steps. Unable to knock with Edith in my arms, I kicked the wood.

No servants responded.

I shifted Edith a little higher and kicked the door again. Holding her this close was pure torture. When she'd sat stiff as a board, her resistance made it easier to pretend the moment meant nothing, but when she melted into me and dropped her precious head against my shoulder, the warmth, the weight of her trust branded itself on my soul.

I brushed a kiss to the top of her head then froze, hoping she hadn't felt the gesture through the puffy hairstyle she wore.

I slammed my toes against the door, shooting agony up my leg. *Someone answer this door before I lose control.*

A footman appeared, and I barreled past him, intent on the stairs.

My landlady's door burst open. "I do not allow ladies in men's chambers, Mr. Beauchamp." Her strident voice halted me and brought much needed clarity to my mind.

What was I doing carrying Edith to my chambers?

I sucked in a deep breath. This was what came of allowing myself to dwell on Edith's inappropriate suggestion to visit. When I saw her in danger, my mind scrambled. I put no thought into my actions. Except the one thing I'd dreamed of since yesterday.

Fantasies of Edith never ended well. I knew that. Should have controlled myself.

Her esteemed Mr. Lucas wouldn't have lost himself in delusions. *You'll never measure up to him.*

"Bring her into my sitting room," Mrs. Clay's voice softened. "I'll care for the poor dear."

Relief filled me. The strict but kind widow, whose reduced circumstances had forced her to take on boarders, would take good care of my Edith.

"Mr. Beauchamp." Mrs. Howard slapped a hand against the closing door, startling the footman and me. She forced her way in and gasped out, "You must stop. Think of her reputation. I thought you were taking us to the carriage. We cannot be here."

I suppressed a groan. Why hadn't I thought of their carriage?

"Mrs. Clay has kindly offered us the use of her sitting room." I nodded at my landlady. "Perhaps—since we are already here—it might be best to tend Edith's injuries while a servant fetches the carriage."

Mrs. Howard hesitated.

"Mrs. Clay is a lady. My mother would never let me rent from anyone less."

That sealed her approval, but Mrs. Howard still scorched me with a glare as she brushed past.

I followed her into Mrs. Clay's rooms and placed Edith on the reclining sofa. I backed away just in time to bump into Edith's sister.

"What were you thinking?" Susanne hissed.

"I wasn't thinking."

"If that isn't the truth." She tsked. "You never did where Edith was concerned."

'Twas true. Edith always flipped me upside down. I rubbed the back of my neck.

"I didn't mean any harm."

"No, I don't imagine you did. Like when you left her."

At her bitter tone, my gaze jerked to Susanne. She always treated me cordially when we crossed paths during the summer months. Where did this animosity spring from?

"Susanne, stop fussing and come help." Whether Mrs. Howard meant to rescue me or not, I appreciated it all the same.

A movement caught my eye. The door to Mrs. Clay's private sitting room gaped open. Servants gaggled around, stretching to see the commotion.

"You, there." I pointed at a young lad.

He flinched at being caught, then snapped to attention. "Aye, sir."

I tossed him a coin with orders to find the Howards' carriage and have the coachman bring it round. "Tell him Clarence Beauchamp sent you."

The lad disappeared in a hurry, and I shut the door on the remaining gapers.

Which left me with my vigil to return to. Watching them care for Edith burned when I longed for the privilege. But it was for the best. I lost all sense in her presence, especially when I touched her. Always had.

After seeing them home, I would not call upon Edith to inquire after her health no matter what gentlemanly protocols demanded. We needed distance between us. A lot of distance.

An itch broke out in my chest. I didn't want space. Longing swept in, hard and fast.

I required an occupation to divert my mind, my heart before I went mad. But what?

Mrs. Clay opened a cupboard. The squeak of the hinge reminded me of the bird, and Edith's desire to see it today. Why not fetch her fledgling? It might bring a smile to her lips.

I bounded up the steps to my two-pair of stairs rooms. The greedy creature chirped away in the cage Mrs. Clay had insisted I purchase. I threw a fresh cone into the cage, hoping to quiet the thing.

I returned downstairs, but no one noticed my entrance, not even Edith.

Now I stood around, useless, with a bird cage. Why had I thought this a brilliant idea?

You are a fool, Clarence. You always were.

Then the bird chirped.

Chapter Five

E ach chirp of the bird rang like a proverbial knell of the man's
prediction. 'The world will end! The world will end!' Over and
over again it chirped.

The robust, healthy sound ought to be a benediction. I had saved
something. But the bands squeezed all the tighter around my chest.
Why had I decided saving a bird would give me a sense of absolution?
It was too small, too insignificant.

The bird called again, 'The world will end.'

I could barely breathe.

In the year of the earthquakes, when panicked Londoners and
pompous clergymen proclaimed a third quake would swallow the
city on April 4th, 1750, Mother became overwrought and forced us
to sew earthquake gowns.

The extra layers in our skirts kept us warm through the night
we spent in a field outside London watching to see if the city would
fall. Clarence and I treated it as naught but a lark, frolicking about
unperturbed while Mother sat in the carriage fraying the lace of her
sleeves.

But I could not brush off today's prediction. Not after the
harshest winter anyone remembered, and not after nearly meeting
my Maker.

What a pitiful account my life added up to: a pile of moderately done needlework, frippery purchased, calls made and returned, numerous balls and dinners where I found no husband...and one saved bird. All sure to burn along with the wood, hay, and stubble mentioned somewhere in the Bible.

So much hardship this winter. Gardeners dressed as mourners had walked in a procession through the streets, begging lest they starve because the ground lay too frozen for them to work. And that one lady...

A shiver raced over my skin at the grim end of Anne Sizer.

She'd gone to buy bread. An ordinary task until she wandered into a boggy fen and never made it home. Just as I nearly didn't make it home today.

Mother rubbed liniment into my palm and a burning sensation flashed up my arms. Was this what Anne felt? Did one feel it as they froze to death?

My stomach twisted.

"Edith?" Mother's tender voice cut through the horrifying images in my head.

"Yes, Mother?"

"How is your hand?"

I blinked my wrapped limb into focus. I'd missed most of her ministrations, lost in my own head.

"Is something wrong? Do I need to try wrapping it again?" Mother reached for my hand.

"It's fine." Or as fine as an appendage could be when it felt on fire. I took a deep breath. "Do you ever wonder about the end of the world?"

Mother jerked back. "Wh-Why would you ask me that?" Her voice trembled.

"There was this fellow in the marketplace—"

"You shouldn't listen to street preachers." Clarence's voice snapped. "Mr. Bell is a menace. He's one of those Methodists."

How did he know who spoke to me? Not that the man had addressed himself as Mr. Bell, but Clarence seemed so confident of the fellow's identity.

"Do you hear me, Edith?"

I kept my silence, unwilling to poison them with the darkness which had plagued me through the winter. So much suffering.

"You listen to Mr. Beauchamp," Mrs. Clay added her opinion.

Which started Clarence up again. "Methodists are heretics, all of them, but even the man's own leader has renounced Mr. Bell's claims—in the newssheets no less."

Oh, he'd read of the man in the papers.

"You have nothing to fear. Think no more on it."

But his words couldn't quiet the helplessness swelling within, nor silence the bird he held in the cage.

I looked at Mother. She knew what it was to wonder, to worry, but she wouldn't meet my gaze as she fingered her lace cuff.

A knock at the door drew Clarence away.

A servant boy said our carriage had arrived.

I shooed the hens around me, but they clucked, fussed, and decided Clarence ought to carry me to the carriage. No one asked if I could walk or if I even wanted to be carried again.

My former friend set down the birdcage and scooped me into his arms. "I have you."

His words, so reminiscent of my assurances to the bird yesterday, brought a sense of comfort. My annoyance frizzled. It was nice to be cared for.

Until he rapped my head against the carriage when he tried to thread me through the carriage door. Light flared, turning the world hazy.

Poor distraught Clarence. He apologized, fussed, and nearly slipped his fingers into my hair to check for an injury then seemed to think better of it at the last moment. His hands hovered mid-air, neither touching me nor withdrawing.

"I'm fine."

"Are you sure?" His dear, worried gaze probed mine. His hands remained at the ready.

Hm. "You have brown eyes."

He blinked those warm orbs a few times, as if startled, then he withdrew to a more respectable distance and reached for a lap rug.

"Indeed." He smoothed the rug over my lap, then seemed to realize my legs lay underneath and snatched his hands back. "I beg your pardon."

"Thank you, Mr. Beauchamp," Mother said, breaking the awkward moment.

Clarence assisted Mother and Susanne into the carriage, closed the door, and shot one more concerned glance my way before the horses jerked into motion.

Then the wheels took up the chant from the bird. Every rattle over a cobblestone echoed, 'The world will end.'

But I wasn't ready for it to end.

Chapter Six

I tightened my fist until my knuckles cracked. I itched to hit someone. Highly unacceptable behavior at a ball, but the lot of these gentlemen were lunatics.

In all the years I stayed away, burying myself in books and law, I never imagined the scene occurring before my very eyes.

Edith only danced with old codgers and simpering fools. How could the good men of London be blind to her delicate allures?

Nigh on a fortnight had passed since I held Edith in my arms, and it still haunted me.

"Why, pray tell," the voice of Edith's brother slurred near my ear, "do you look like you wish to murder my sister? What has she done to you now?"

"Nay. 'Tis not Edith I wish to throttle. Why do the gentlemen not seek her hand?"

"Ah." Archibald nodded. "That is your fault, I fear."

"Mine?"

"It was widely reported you had an understanding with her. La, half the time I thought you did."

I flexed my fingers. "Your sister didn't."

He inclined his head. "Nonetheless, society generally acknowledged it as so, then you cried off before her debut. There must be something wrong with her."

"It wasn't like that."

"Gossip is seldom based on fact."

He couldn't be right. Was he? "That was years ago."

"Society does not forget. Besides, she's an old maid now."

"Balderdash. Edith doesn't look a day older than when she came out of the schoolroom."

"Be blind all you like, but my sister's no girl anymore and never was much of a catch if you ask me."

I shot him a glare for saying such a hateful thing.

Archie shrugged and surveyed the room. A beat of silence surrounded us until he said, "I imagine the way she used to look past all the other men as if searching for someone else didn't help her cause either."

No doubt she'd searched for her perfect Mr. Lucas since I failed to provide their introduction. I gritted my teeth. "Surely, you introduced her to men."

He snorted and sloshed his drink. "I would never encourage a match betwixt a sister of mine and any fellows whose company I keep. They're not the suitable sorts."

I eyed the dissolute man. Hm, perhaps, it was better he hadn't fulfilled his brotherly duties. But that did not mean Archibald could not be of use to me.

My parents' servants had brought an alarming report to my attention. One of such magnitude I broke my vow not to attend a ball Edith attended, but she need not know of my presence here if her brother discreetly put my mind at ease.

"I understand your sister might have given credence to a street preacher's whims about the world ending. Is there any truth to that?"

"First I've heard of it."

Relief soaked into me. The next time my parents' servants brought fresh pinecones from Mr. Howard's tree for Chirp-in, I'd scold them soundly.

Well, after I interrogated them about Edith's welfare. They'd be less loose with their tongue if I scolded them first. And I lived off their secondhand information.

"But then," Archibald said, "I haven't been home since January. You'd best speak with Edith." He wandered off, spilling some of his drink.

My relief shattered. I'd much rather hide on the other side of the ballroom than seek out his sister.

Pearls adorned her angelic hair tonight. And sometime in the last few years, she'd mastered the art of the fan, fluttering it with a captivating grace. Ugh, I still behaved the besotted fool around her.

But Archibald was right. I needed to speak with Edith. Only, we'd have to dance to gain the privacy required for a conversation about Mr. Bell.

My stomach dipped. Oh, I wanted to dance with Edith. Forget my questions about Mr. Bell, I wanted to glory in her.

The first step proved hardest, then I didn't let myself stop or question the wisdom of my actions until I stood behind her.

"E—" I choked on her Christian name. Proper etiquette was required here. "Miss Howard?"

She spun, surprise spreading across her face.

"Will you do me the honor of dancing the next with me?"

Her eyes widened. "You wish to dance with me?"

"I do." Desperately had for years. A proper dance, not the bumbling moments when I taught her to dance. Even if I treasured those memories.

She stood there blinking at me until her mother nudged her arm.

Edith gave a little jump as she came to herself. She looked from her mother to my outstretched hand and slowly placed her hand in mine.

I told myself not to take this to heart as I led her onto the dance floor, but the silly organ tripled in size until I thought it might burst from my chest.

The music began, and I almost forgot the steps. Blood thrummed through my body. My hands trembled at every contact with my love. And when her grey orbs shyly met mine, a jolt slammed through me.

Utter bliss.

Until I caught sight of the shadows in her eyes. That putrid jar of questions still lay between us. I couldn't ask her about Mr. Bell, didn't even dare speak lest the jar topple over.

My joy soured. How much of the dance could we go without speaking?

Yet the charged silence possessed its own kind of torture.

We made it to the second dance of the set before she said, "You like wigs now." It wasn't a question.

I missed a step. "I'm not wearing a wig." Hadn't even powdered my hair because I knew she'd hate it.

"No, but barristers do."

"I tolerate wigs more than like them."

"Then, why pursue law?"

"I enjoy the work."

She flattened her lips.

I scrambled for something to say now that the silence lay broken. I needed to direct the conversation. Keep it away from undesirable topics. I excelled at this in the courtroom, could control judges and witnesses with ease, but my mind resembled a ravished dinner plate. Not enough scraps left for a single bite.

I knew her injuries had healed, thanks to the gossiping servants. Besides, 'twould be best to stick to statements not questions. Which ruled out Mr. Bell. What else might we discuss?

I hesitated too long.

"How many balls have you spent watching me and never speaking to me?" An undercurrent of anger ripped through the thin sheet of her polite smile.

"None." I resisted the urge to tuck my feet under me, lest she stomp on my toes like she had a time or two in our youth.

"How many?"

"This is the first."

"You expect me to believe that? You've been in London for years, Clarence. Or should I call you Mr. Beauchamp?"

"Please don't."

"We barely know each other."

"You know everything important about me." Well, except for that one thing.

"Then why did you stay away?" And there it was. That one thing.

"Mr. Lucas." I choked out his name. The man she requested I investigate while attending Cambridge alongside him.

"What does he have to do with anything?"

"He has everything to do with it."

I'd foolishly agreed to her plan, assuming Mr. Lucas would be as full of flaws as his guardian, the not-so-honorable Henry Fox. But Mr. Lucas was kind, even-tempered, tolerated no vices, and managed his impressive inheritance with a wisdom I admired. If I hadn't wanted to marry Edith, I couldn't have chosen a better match for her.

Which proved she knew exactly what she was doing. Knew what sort of man she ought to wed, wanted to wed, and it wasn't me.

So, I stayed away. Lest I fall at her feet and beg her to choose me. Dignity be cast aside. Oh, how I had loved her. Still loved her. "You made your choice, Edith. I was trying to honor that." And not make a fool of myself.

She frowned. "My choice? What choice?"

I gritted my teeth, unwilling to speak the man's name again. "Leave it be. Please, just leave it be."

We lasted a few more steps in silence before she asked, "Were we friends?" Her soft, broken voice cut me asunder.

"Of course. How could you ask such a thing?"

"You called me your bane. And you never came back."

"No, that's not why. Never think that."

"Then what should I think?" Her wide innocent eyes plagued me. "Why did you leave?"

Old fears consumed me. I couldn't do this. Not in so public a place where all could witness my humiliation should she laugh this time as she had the only time I confessed my love to her.

"Please, I beg you. Do not... Do not make me declare myself. Not here."

"Then when? Where?" She discreetly spread her hands before resuming the dance. "Will you ever tell me why you left?"

She hadn't even caught my slip about declaring myself.

I was drowning, choking, and once more a young lad of fourteen. Heady after a dance lesson, I'd blurted out, *Edith, I love you. I always have.*

And she'd laughed. *'Oh, Clarence, my prince will say something ever so much cleverer than that when he declares his love.'*

Chapter Seven

The melted mess before me little resembled Mr. Negri's excellent ices, but the fault lay not with the distinguished confectioner of the Pot and Pineapple. I had dragged my spoon round and round the coffee flavored delicacy until it returned to its pre-frozen state. All the while, Susanne blathered about one thing after another.

And I didn't care. Truth be told, I hadn't wanted to come. The cold, wet sweetmeat reminded me how Clarence froze at the ball four days ago. The dance had ended, sparing Clarence the embarrassment of being caught. Not that I'd been spared such humiliation when he abruptly returned me to my mother and left the ball without speaking to another soul.

How the whispers flew over that.

And yet, I didn't care. I just wanted answers, but I'd neither seen nor heard from Clarence since. Would he ever explain why he'd left?

"You aren't listening, Edith."

I jerked my head up to meet my sister's steady gaze. "I beg your pardon."

"Has he hurt you again?" She reached out and took my hand.

"Who?"

"Clarence Beauchamp. Who else?" Susanne's brow furrowed.

Who else indeed. "He won't tell me why he left. Begged me not to make him 'declare himself.'"

She gave a little squeal of delight. "He said that? What did you say?"

I blinked. "Nothing. I said nothing. He was talking gibberish about Mr. Lucas and my choice."

"George Lucas of Parham House?"

I nodded.

"Why would he talk about Mr. Lucas?"

"I don't know."

She tapped her empty bowl. "I've always wondered, did you two quarrel before he went away to Cambridge?"

"No. I asked him for his help with my debut and if he'd introduce me to Mr. Lucas."

"Edith." Susanne's shocked tone carried through the Pot and the Pineapple.

"Keep your voice down." I glared at her.

"How could you ask him such a thing?"

"Why shouldn't I?"

"Surely, you must know." She tilted her head meaningfully.

I looked at her blankly.

She huffed. "When you were barely out of the schoolroom, it was perhaps understandable, but you cannot be so simple-minded now. You must know."

Know what? "Stop talking in riddles."

"He was in love with you."

"Clarence," I said his name to be sure we spoke of the same man, "loved me?"

"Most ardently."

"But he never said anything. He even agreed to help me with my debut."

"He did?"

I nodded.

"That is puzzling."

"If he loved me—"

"There is no question." Susanne interrupted. "He adored you."

"How can you be sure? He never said so."

"Oh, Edith." Pity painted across her features. "There are a thousand ways a man betrays his heart. I knew it the day he walked away from a game of marbles, just because you said you needed his help."

"What does that have to do with love?"

"Do you not remember how obsessed he was with marbles? He even refused to go inside for meals until he finished a game."

"I don't remember that."

She pinched her lips as if she thought I lied, then questions slowly trickled into her eyes. "I suppose it's possible... You might not..."

Could she finish a sentence? I barely restrained from drumming my fingers on the table.

She leaned in close and placed her hand over mine, as if speaking to an ignorant child. "He left every game the moment you walked past asking him to do whatever it was you wanted. For the rest of us—yea, even food placed second to marbles—but not you. Never you."

My mind skated back. Far back in time. Clarence played with marbles from the nursery until well after attending boarding school. A few times, I hadn't interrupted his game, just watched, wondering what made him play with such intensity, his eyes aglow. Rather keen over each shot. Passionate even. His attention unwavering.

Until he noticed my presence. Then he lost all his skill, fumbling and turning red when he missed. Scuffing his shoes around in the dirt. Stealing glances my way. But he'd fumbled and blushed no matter what he was doing.

"That's love?"

"Oh, Edith, he adored you. And I strongly suspect he still does."

My world tilted. "Then why did he agree to help me with Mr. Lucas?"

"You're certain he agreed?"

"Completely."

Susanne shook her head, as lost as me. "It's very strange."

Baffling even.

"I'd like to go home." I pushed away from the table, leaving my melted ices untasted.

"Of course." Susanne scrambled to her feet and threaded her arm through mine. Her support brought much needed comfort after her startling revelation. Clarence loved me?

The street, nay, my whole world was a blur until Susanne muttered. "Must he be here?"

I blinked, and an overrun Berkeley Square came into focus.

A street preacher stood in the midst of a hostile crowd.

Susanne steered us away, but I stopped, an unsatiable curiosity bubbling within. Clarence tried to blame this on the Methodists, but 'twas our clergymen who had proclaimed the end of the world in 1750. How did they determine their predictions? What would happen when the Lord returned? Was He returning in just under a fortnight? So many questions pressed for release.

But this wasn't the same preacher as before. The clothes of this one bespoke gentlemanly grace and something in his manner too—the words he chose, and the quiet dignity which surrounded him. His face shone with an earnestness, and his voice carried with authority over the jeering crowd. "Are you ready to meet your Maker?"

"Are you, mister?" A man threw something at the back of the preacher's head.

I yelled and pointed, but too late. The hard object met its target with a sickening thud.

The preacher crumpled to the ground.

The crowd laughed, and a few others threw various objects at the fallen man.

I pulled out of Susanne's clutches and rushed to the stranger's aid.

"Sir? Sir, are you hurt?" I fell to my knees beside the man.

A few stray items hit me, but nothing as harmful as the blood covered rock lying beside the preacher.

Susanne screeched at the crowd and shamed them into dropping their missiles and dispersing with surprising swiftness.

The preacher tried to stand but wobbled and sat down, holding the back of his head. "I do believe I might need a moment. My sincerest apologies, madam."

"Think no more of it. Shall we fetch a physician? How badly are you hurt?" I wanted to peel his hand away and check his wound, but some rules of etiquette cannot be broken. Even when they chafe.

Now, had Clarence been sitting there...

My breath left me. The thought of Clarence suffering an injury made my pulse spike. I gulped and willed the image away.

Susanne leaned close and whispered in my ear. "Edith, we don't know him. You cannot sit on the ground next to him. Stand up." She tugged on my arm.

She had a point. I stood. "I'm Edith Howard."

"Edith!"

My sister was wearing out my name today.

"You said we don't know him. I'm introducing myself."

"You can't do that."

"I don't see anyone here who can supply a proper introduction, and he plainly needs assistance. We cannot leave him here."

Her lips twisted as if she desired to do just that.

My glare shamed her into relinquishing.

"I'll see if I can find help." Susanne moved away.

I faced the preacher. "How is your head?"

"The throbbing lessens if I keep still. Please do not think ill of me that I do not honor you by standing or looking into your face."

"Do not fear on my account. I am not offended."

We waited quietly while Susanne's inquiries met with wide-eyed stares and vigorous headshakes.

The street preacher asked, "Why do you not back away from me like the others?"

"I heard one of you, another man, say something. I haven't been able to put it from my mind."

"What did he say?"

"That the world will end."

"Ah." He didn't say anything further, but something negative niggled in his response.

"You do not believe it is true? Were you not saying so a moment ago?"

"I believe our Lord's return to be imminent, but I presume this other fellow gave you a date?"

"The twenty-eighth."

"That I do not believe."

"Why not?"

"The Bible says we cannot know the day nor the hour. 'Twould be my honor to show you the verse, if you're of a mind to learn."

A spark shot through my chest. "I would."

Now, how to convince Susanne this man must go home with us?

"Hatfield, by the by." The gentleman slowly leaned his head back and squinted, either at the sun above or because of the pain in his head. "Andrew Hatfield at your service."

Chapter Eight

In Matthew chapter four, Jesus preached, 'Repent: for the kingdom of heaven is at hand.'

I grimaced and cast a furtive look about my club. So far no one had noticed my unusual reading material. Hopefully, it stayed that way.

'Twas nigh on a sennight after the ball, and Edith hadn't given up on the end of the world. I needed a verse to set her aright. Then perhaps I could face her, putting that disaster of a ball behind us.

Just not that verse. I turned the page.

"Edith's converted you too, eh, Clarence?" Archibald's voice came from behind my chair.

I jerked, nearly spilling the Bible. "Don't be absurd." I smoothed the holy pages. "I'm gathering evidence to convince your sister Mr. Bell belongs in Bedlam."

It had to be here somewhere. Jesus hadn't come for centuries.

An odd discomfort broke out on my chest, the same weighty itch which afflicted me whenever the clergy preached on this topic.

"Have you found it?" Archie sat nearby.

"Not entirely." I rubbed my chest. "Wesley quoted a verse I recognized in his first letter to the editor. Something about no man knowing the day or hour." I rifled through a stack of papers and pulled out the January tenth edition. I tapped a finger on Wesley's few lines. "He failed to mention the reference, but 'tis one of the Gospels, I'm certain."

"And you've taken it upon yourself to find the quote?" Archie picked up the newspaper.

One would think that obvious. "Aye." I returned to the gospel of Matthew.

My inquiries to the clergy had reaped only mutterings of 'insane, radical, and heathen.' No evidence, no verse to disprove Mr. Bell. Not even the one Wesley mentioned.

Perhaps they didn't wish to incriminate their fellow clergymen who, in 1750, had proclaimed the same erroneous message as Bell did now.

"Have you given any consideration Mr. Bell may be right?" Archie asked.

I twisted his direction. "You cannot be serious."

He shrugged. "Bell is a member of the Methodist society. Their leader is a legitimate clergyman who preaches in churches all over England. No one puts a stop to it."

"They ought to, and furthermore..." I shifted the sheets again and pulled out Wesley's second letter to the editor, passing it to Archibald. "Mr. Bell has left the society."

Archie skimmed the article. "Little wonder after Wesley called him deluded in the first letter."

"Indeed." I attempted to read the Bible again, but Archie wasn't finished bothering me.

"May I be of assistance?"

Oh, not such a bother then.

"By all means." I waved a hand at the shelf housing the holy tomes.

I'd never understood why a gentleman's club provided such a vast array of religious books, unless for a show of piety none of the members felt, but a barrister valued good resources. Hence why I read here instead of at home. Plus, no chirping birds abode at the club.

Archibald fetched a Bible and barely began reading before he reached for the quill and paper I'd set out.

"Found something?"

He nodded and scratched out a reference with a steady hand. Since when did Archie have a steady hand?

I eyed him closely. He was sober. I couldn't remember the last time I'd seen him thus.

Archibald read aloud, "'For when they shall say, Peace and safety; then sudden destruction cometh upon them...'"

He read on, but that first part sounded eerily like Mr. Bell's prediction. Had Archibald forgotten our objective to disprove the man?

I shook off the disturbing words and returned to my task.

I came to Matthew six. Jesus prayed, 'Thy kingdom come.' How oft had I repeated those words and never meant them? Never wanted or expected Him. I rather liked my life the way it was.

The itch or weight or whatever it was pressed harder, wider. I shifted in my seat.

Time and chapters ticked passed, and Archibald's list of urgent warnings grew. My side stayed blank.

My throat tightened. So many passages on His kingdom. I almost choked on them until reaching Matthew chapter twenty-four verse thirty-six.

"Eureka!" I bolted upright. "'But of that day and hour knoweth no *man*, no, not the angels of heaven, but my Father only.' Surely, this will convince your sister Mr. Bell spews lies. One cannot know the date."

Which on a technicality meant this verse belonged on Archie's side of the list.

I shoved that thought away.

"Sorry, old chap, but the Methodist preacher already told her that one."

"I beg your pardon. Who now?"

"Some clergy-fellow, calls himself Hatfield. Edith brought him home, and they pored over these passages." He swished the quill at the list. "How else do you think an old sot like me knows all these? Hatfield proved a font of information before Father came home and threw him out of the house."

Heat surged through my veins. "Edith consorted with a Methodist?"

"Eh?" Archibald looked up, belatedly noticing my building fury. "Ah, yes, right nice chap, he's mostly convinced Edith Christ isn't returning on the twenty-eighth. Or maybe he hasn't because Edith remains firm that He is coming. Mother's gone mad like she did in 1750, and Father's livid about it all. Been quite the row at our place."

I needed to see Edith.

The room blurred long before I realized my feet moved at a rapid clip.

"Best hurry," Archibald called after me. "Father's taking Edith to the country, far away from all the mad Methodists. They were packing when I left not an hour ago. Might have even left already."

Chapter Nine

"Street preachers are dangerous," Clarence seethed.

"In the case of Mr. Bell, I would have to agree, but that does not follow all are so."

His jaw flexed. His eyes burned with a thousand unspoken words, but I remained firm. Our Lord could return at any moment, whether today, tomorrow, or some other day. We must be prepared for an imminent return. The Bible taught us so. It had nothing to do with misguided Mr. Bell.

Clarence sucked in a deep breath. "You truly are my bane."

"Because I won't agree with you?"

He rubbed his face. "That's not why."

"Then tell me why."

"You know why."

"Because you supposedly love me?"

"Supposedly? You doubt it?" Hurt marred his expression.

"You have never said you love me. Others have, but not you. There is a mild implication with your words and sly looks, but I don't believe it. A man in love doesn't scream at the girl that she's his bane." I almost spat the words at him. Most unladylike, but I was sick of the way he blustered and yelled. "He doesn't leave her, abandon her after years of friendship. Nay." I shook my head. "You do not love me."

He jerked as if slapped. His eyes slid shut, and little lines of pain feathered out from them. "You're right." He scuffed a hand through his hair. "I'm sorry, Edith."

He knocked several locks loose from the queue at the nape of his neck, and I swallowed the urge to smooth his hair back into place.

My stomach swooped. Since when did I long to touch Clarence's hair?

He took a deep breath, opened his eyes, and focused on me. Those warm brown depths pulled me from my wayward thoughts.

"I do love you, Edith. This is perhaps not the place nor the time to declare it. And you are right. I have not behaved as a man in love. I ran. I hid in fear of rejection. I'm a coward and a sorry lover. But love you I have, ardently and constantly. I can no more deny it than to deny my own heartbeat—and God knows I've tried to forget you. You are under my skin for better or for worse."

He stepped closer and my mouth dried at his nearness, his passion.

"I'm sorry I left. You made a good choice. Mr. Lucas is an excellent gentleman, and I hated myself for liking him, but like him I did. Still do." He swallowed. "I should have kept my promise and at least told you that and then pleaded with you to choose me instead. Come what may, I ought to have been honest." His gaze dropped to the ground. "If I ruined things for you and Mr. Lucas, I apologize."

Of all the effrontery. "I haven't thought of that man in years, Clarence. I certainly never looked, never hoped for Mr. Lucas or any other gentleman." Blood pounded in my ears. "I didn't strain my neck at every street corner or scour a ballroom trying to spot their profile. My heart never fell when they failed to show. I never hoped to the point of begging one of them would be there when I dined at his parents' house."

He blinked at my last words, as if catching their meaning.

"I never cared about any of them." The words tore from my throat at an unladylike volume, from a place so deep naught but a yell could have dragged it to the surface. "I looked for you, Clarence. I only wanted you."

My words filled the room like a thunderclap, shredding the veil over my own heart and laying it bare. How had I not known? All this time. All these years.

I loved Clarence.

I dearly, deeply loved this oaf blinking at me. And he thought his love obvious.

A riot of emotions chased across his face, tentative hope leading the charge. "In what way did you look for me? The way I longed for you?" He shuttered his feelings. "Or did you look for your friend?"

Joy and relief burst within. To know oneself is freedom. I laughed. How I loved this blockhead! I opened my mouth to tell him, but a gruff voice cut me off.

"We're leaving." Father smashed the golden glow around me. His fingers—like iron bands—clamped around my elbow. He pulled hard toward the door.

"Father?" I stumbled and struggled to keep my feet under me.

"It's time."

We'd been stepping into the carriage when Clarence arrived out of breath and begging for an audience with me. Father agreed to a ten-minute delay but no more. Surely, the time had not passed already. We'd barely started talking, and we had so much still to say.

"If I could have a few minutes more. I promise, Father, just a few."

"No." Father dragged me from our sitting room.

"Please, Father."

He ignored me.

"Clarence!"

My call jolted Clarence from his stupor. He dashed into the hallway after us. "Sir? Please, sir. Wait."

But Father didn't slacken his pace.

I reached for my beloved with my free hand. Our fingertips brushed, but Father jerked my arm. We lost contact.

"Clarence." My voice broke.

His eyes wild, Clarence chased after us, begging Father to stop, but his pleas landed on deaf ears.

Father dragged me out the door, down the steps, and shoved me into the carriage. He clambered in after me and slammed the door.

"Please, sir." Clarence's voice came muffled from without. He yanked on the handle, but Father held the door shut and ordered the coachman to take off.

A crack sounded through the air. Was it my heart or the coachmen's whip?

Clarence struggled to stay abreast of us. For all his wonderful attributes, he wasn't trained like the footmen to run alongside a carriage. He lost hold of the door.

"Please, sir! I must know her answer."

Father let down the side glass just long enough to yell, "She laughed, Clarence. Nothing could be clearer. She doesn't love you." His words slammed into my beloved, stopping him as nothing else could.

Horror washed over me, freezing my reaction a few beats too long.

Clarence fell from view.

"No." I clawed at Father's shoulder. Urgency propelled me across him, but he prevented my access to the window.

"Please, Father, I love him."

"You don't think I know that?"

I stilled. "Then why did you tell him otherwise?"

"I thought if anyone could convince you to abandon this 'end of the world' nonsense, it would be Clarence. But no, a moment more and he'd have begged for your hand."

"Why is that a problem?" It sounded wonderful. I twisted my neck to see out the little window in the rear of the carriage.

Clarence stood in the middle of the street, head downcast, shoulders drooped.

Look at me. But the fog of defeat wrapped too thickly around him. London swallowed him as our wheels rattled on.

"He had to be stopped," Father said, "before he ruined everything."

"What could Clarence have possibly ruined?" I turned back to my father.

He cast a harried glance at Mother. She scratched a red patch on her neck, unaware and unable to stop the nervous action. How could I have foreseen bringing the Methodist preacher home would incite Mother to abandon her cuffs and attack her own skin? The hives had spread from her arms to all over her. She rarely slept anymore.

I hadn't meant to drive her into this dark place.

If only my parents understood one didn't need to fear the end of the world. As long as one prepared themselves, it could be a joyous occasion. Like waiting for a wedding.

Which reminded me of Clarence. What did Mother's nerves have to do with him? "I don't understand."

"If you deny this end of the world business, I'll turn the carriage around."

Cold splashed over me. Father didn't mean... He wouldn't.

But his steely gaze confirmed my worst fears. He meant to use Clarence against me.

After Mother's nerves snapped, I'd tried to keep silent for her sake, but Father shouted at me to deny my Lord's return. Mother couldn't recover unless I recanted. A quiet difference of opinion would not do.

And now he dangled Clarence before me.

How could he demand such a thing? My devotion for Christ threaded as deeply through my veins as my love for Clarence. I couldn't deny one or the other. My heart rent at the thought.

"As I suspected." Father settled back into the carriage seat, face impassive.

I wanted to scream I hadn't made my choice, but I couldn't recant. Oh, if I only had the freedoms sons enjoyed! A daughter could not choose her own path.

I glanced out the little window, but Clarence was gone.

I'll write, my love. I'll write and tell you all that's in my heart.

Little comfort a letter offered him now.

A knife plunged into my chest. How could I have stood there professing Christ's return at any moment when I failed to apply the principle behind the belief? What if Christ did return? What if I died at the hands of highwaymen on the journey home? What if Clarence never learned how much I loved him?

A foulness stung my tongue. And no matter how hard I gulped, "what if" tasted so bitter.

Chapter Ten

My thoughts plagued me like an insatiable baby bird while my shoes beat a weary rhythm on the streets of London. Footfall after absentminded footfall on the twenty-eighth day of February, exactly one week after Mr. Howard tore Edith from me. We'd know one way or another tonight who was right.

But then Edith said she believed our Lord could come at any moment, not necessarily this day.

I didn't know what I believed anymore. It all jumbled in my head. The doubts, the sense of urgency in the Bible, the certainty when the clergy spoke of Christ's return, and my fear we all looked like fools for still believing in an event which hadn't occurred for the last several centuries.

I ground my teeth. I hated looking like a fool.

I swiped a hand down my face and looked at the sky. 'Twas darkening, not blue or grey with clouds as I expected. How long had I been walking?

I studied my surroundings. Unfamiliar buildings cast long shadows. It took a moment to place myself—Spitalfields. I'd wandered far from home.

Sounds of a large crowd drew my attention ahead and I walked on.

"Prepare to meet thy Maker," a voice boomed and stopped my feet cold.

The officials must have missed one of Bell's followers when they arrested the troublemaker and his supporters yesterday on the mound near St. Luke's hospital. 'For disturbing the peace,' they'd said. A fitting charge. I hadn't known a moment's peace since Mr. Bell spewed his lies at Edith.

I balled my hands and stepped forward, ready to protect this crowd from the vile man they gathered around. But the preacher largely expounded on the absurdity of claiming Jesus would come today.

The steam seeped out of me as the man—obviously a Methodist—spoke against one of their former members and said nothing I could gainsay.

"May I be of assistance, good sir?" a voice said beside me.

I turned to see a clergyman at my elbow. Probably another one of those Methodists.

He smiled, even though I scowled at him. "I can see you are deep in contemplation. Is there perhaps a question I might endeavor to answer?"

I pulled away from the noisy crowd. "You are a Methodist?"

"I am." He held out his hand. "Hatfield at your service."

"Hatfield?"

"You've heard of me?" A quizzical line popped up on his brow.

"You spoke with Miss Howard."

"Ah, on Bruton Street. Delightful creature and quite sincere in her faith."

"How could you pull her away from the church?"

"I wasn't aware I did such a thing."

"She believes Jesus is returning."

"Tonight? I thought I convinced her against that."

"Today or another day, she says it matters not when. She's convinced He's coming."

He cocked his head. "And you are not?"

I wanted to refute him. I wanted to spit in his face, but a mountain of verses proclaiming Christ's second coming stood between us.

Hatfield began to pull out a small volume from one of the pockets of his greatcoat. "May I show you in the Bible—"

"Put that away." I waved a dismissive hand at him. "I've read them all." They hadn't helped.

He paused, book half out. "And yet you do not believe."

I clenched my teeth until they ached. One swift punch to his jaw and his head would snap back, so satisfying. But, nay, I could not indulge the impulse. How irksome gentlemanly rules of conduct could be. "I don't know what to believe."

"Perhaps, I can help with that."

"I should not be speaking with you. You'll lead me away from the church."

He returned his Bible to its pocket. "A common misconception. Wesley"—he nodded at the street preacher—"is a firm supporter of the church. Insists we ought to be in our parish pews on Sunday. For as long as Wesley lives, Methodists will be loyal members of the Church of England."

I inspected the impassioned man before the crowd. So, that was the infamous John Wesley. Interesting.

I turned to Hatfield. "And you? Do you support the church?"

"I should hope so." He let out a chuckle. "I seek a living within it."

I let out a breath of relief.

Many espoused that Wesley employed lay preachers—such as Mr. Bell, nothing but a life-guard man he was—but to seek a living, one must be deemed fit for the position by a university and pass an examination by the bishop. Hatfield was a true clergyman.

"Why not tell us when He'd return?"

"He gave us everything we needed to know. Yea, more than we needed. There will be a trumpet blast, a shout. We'll meet Him in the air, and the dead shall rise first. He's given us signs to watch for. He just asks us to believe Him about when it will happen."

"But God knows the date."

"Aye, the Father does." Hatfield agreed slowly, a question on his forehead.

"Then why a sense of urgency, of immediacy in the Bible when God knew we'd be waiting for centuries?"

"Ah." Hatfield's smile was gentle. "Urgency is the difference between knowing and believing."

"I beg your pardon?"

"What if someone were to tell you that His Majesty plans to visit Spitalfields—"

I snorted.

He cut me a sidelong glance of amusement. "—but our king had not mentioned when he would come. His visit would then be both imminent and urgent, no matter how long one waited."

"Assuming he ever planned to come."

"That is my point. Once you are told, you have knowledge. One must then decide if they will believe the report, which starts with the credibility of the source." Hatfield reached into his greatcoat, and this time I did not stop him from withdrawing his Bible. "We've an infallible source. God Himself told us He will return, but will you believe Him? Believe this." He laid a hand over his Bible.

My conscience pricked as if a hot poker had been jabbed into the fireplace of my thoughts. Like the flames, I lashed back. "I cannot stand around on the street corners waiting for Him. I've court cases, a landlady. People depend on me."

"Did the great men of faith stand around the street corners? Nay, they subdued kingdoms and shut the mouths of lions through faith in a promise they never received." His gaze caught mine with a challenge. "Faith is not idle. It stirs one to action."

I simmered. Why thrust the onus onto my shoulders? God was the One returning. "He should have just told us when He planned to return. Save us from all the confusion and uncertainty."

"'Tis only uncertain if you doubt, if you've lost your faith." His jab stung.

The blaze roared. "I fail to see a reason He couldn't just tell us!"

"Our Lord's oft warnings against complacency seem a compelling argument, yet one could postulate His reasons endlessly, and nothing would change. The root of this issue remains faith, for 'without faith *it is* impossible to please *him*.'"

I knew that verse. 'Twas in the passage of the great men of faith. The ones who believed day after day, month upon year, generation after generation in a promise they never received.

And God counted it as righteousness.

Hatfield was right. On two counts. While I'd catered to many a fickle judge, God never changed. He always required faith. And if I refused to believe what God had told us, nothing—not a date or a reason—would have changed my mind. 'Twas my faith on trial here.

My fire banked and fizzled.

A lifetime was a long time to prepare for an event I might never see. All the while believing it could happen in my next breath.

Now that was faith.

With an intense flash, almost physically bright, I realized I wanted that. Nay, I needed it to please Him, the great Judge Who counted faith more precious than gold.

Forgive my unbelief. Help me.

'For God, who commanded the light to shine out of darkness, hath shined in our hearts, to *give* the light of the knowledge of the glory of God in the face of Jesus Christ.' 2 Corinthians 4:6 KJV

Chapter Eleven

April
    "The queen herself couldn't boast of such a fine fire screen, Miss Howard," the widow called after me, flapping a tatty apron.

I offered her a smile and a wave then twisted around to continue down the lane toward home. I ought to make her a new apron. Well, after I completed the other items on my growing list. So many needs, but they didn't overwhelm me anymore.

'We do our best, and God blesses the rest,' the local parson said. 'Two measly mites gave God more pleasure than all the bags of gold those rich men arrogantly cast into the treasury. 'Tis not the size of the gift which determines its significance. 'Tis the heart of the giver.'

My soul warmed. I'd done my best needlework for the widow. And her beautiful, gracious spirit blessed me as much as I blessed her.

Spring's sunlight brushed my skin and seeped deep into my soul. God would find me watching, waiting, and faithful when He came, my talents not buried in some field.

By most accounts, I ought to be content walking alone on this lane with God. So much of my world had been righted. The parson's long sessions with my parents helped my father stop bristling whenever someone mentioned Christ's return. Mother's hives had disappeared. The lace on her retrimmed sleeves stayed spotless, and she even slept at night.

But Father still stood between me and Clarence.

He'd confessed last week to keeping back my letters, and when I pressed him for permission to write Clarence on the heels of his admission, Father said, "Not yet."

Restlessness stole in, threatening to overspill like yeast loaf left too long. I slipped through the back gate of our garden and swiped at an errant branch of a topiary.

Then regretted the rash action.

Rushing wouldn't help. I pounded the restlessness down and gently tucked the branch where it belonged.

Please, Lord, help me be patient. Soften Father's heart.

My favorite place in the garden, a flat bench under a spreading oak, beckoned me. I walked to it and sat, leaning my head against the trunk. Sunlight flittered through the leaves and danced across my upturned face. I closed my eyes. Dancing reminded me of Clarence, of all those steps I'd taken in his arms imagining those appendages belonged to someone else. What I wouldn't give to have his arms around me once more, to bask in his love.

Longing pinched. Was this how the Shulamite felt when she searched for Solomon and couldn't find him?

I should stop reading Song of Solomon. 'Twasn't helping.

"Edith." Father's call startled me.

I snapped my eyes open.

He shuffled close, hat in hand, his intention clear to join me on the bench.

I scuttled over to give him room.

"I should not have demanded you deny Christ's return nor divided you from Clarence."

"So you said last week when I forgave you." Why bring it up again? Unless he meant to give his permission.

A tiny quiver ran through me.

Father rubbed his leg. "It needed saying again, so you know you have my blessing."

Hope erupted. "I can write Clarence?"

He huffed. "Better than that. You can talk to him." Father raised his voice and called over the tall hedge to our right. "Clarence, you can join us now."

My beloved stepped around the bushes, and my pulse jolted. I ran to him, buried my face into his chest, and wrapped my arms around his body as I imagined the Shulamite did when Solomon came for her.

Clarence's arms enfolded me. Such sweet surrender. Being held by Clarence could not compare to anything.

"I'll leave you to it then." Father's voice faded as he presumably left.

I pulled back. "Clarence—"

He held a finger to my lips. "Please, Edith, let me speak. There is something I must tell you before my courage fails me." He took a step back and wiped his hand down his greatcoat.

Whether to remove the feel of my lips on his finger or sweat on his palm I knew not.

"I believe our Lord is returning at any moment, but I won't be joining the Methodists."

He trembled as if afraid how I might receive this news. He couldn't even look at me.

"I've spent the last few weeks at their meetinghouse, and while I learned much, Bell deceived many. Others now wish to follow a fellow who supported and encouraged Bell. There is much tension and strife. I found no peace there. It's not where I belong. You need to know that before you decide...before we..."

He stopped as if realizing he was getting ahead of himself. He clamped his mouth shut and resolutely stared over my head.

"Clarence." I willed him to look at me.

A muscle jumped in his jaw, but he didn't look.

I reached up and touched the spot. It was smooth with tiny prickles, but I didn't let myself linger.

I pulled his face down. "I don't want to join the Methodists."

"You don't?" His intense gaze snapped to mine.

I took a deep breath and tried to organize my thoughts into words. "It felt as if I was asleep until the Methodists woke me, but they woke me to truths preached in my own church. So, for their service, I shall be forever grateful. But I've no desire to join their society."

Clarence let out a breath. "That's how I feel. You cannot know what a relief it is to hear you say so, darling."

Warmth spread through me. "I do rather like that. Darling." I rolled the endearment around my tongue, enjoying the taste of it. "Much better than being called your bane."

Red brushed his cheeks. "Forgive me? I only called you my bane when I wanted to wring your neck because you didn't see me, didn't see how much I loved you."

"You suffered unrequited love while I attempted to rescue a fledgling? How is the little bird by the by?"

"He's doing well. I brought him with me but left him at the inn. Didn't wish for Chirp-in's incessant noise to interrupt our reunion."

"Chirp-in?"

He gave a bashful shrug. "I always thought I should have called Pepin, Chirp-in."

"Hm. What would you say to calling him Herald instead? Since his delightful little chirps heralded a new life for us?"

"I'd say listen to his chirps for a few days and then tell me if you still call them delightful. But I'll take it under consideration. Now, to return to your accusation against me."

"My accusation?" I chuckled.

"Yes, I suffered most acutely while you risked your life and limb up a tree. My heart lodged in my throat. I thought you were going to break your beautiful neck." He reached out and feathered a fingertip down my neck.

My pulse skipped.

He leaned close and dropped his voice to an intimate whisper. "Very bane-like actions, Edith Howard."

I swallowed. The rush of his nearness so heady. "What if, instead of my bane, you call me beloved like in Song of Solomon?"

"I believe the fellow was the beloved."

Well, that ruined things. I wrinkled my nose at him. "Mayhap I ought to start calling you my bane."

He laughed, but then his mirth faded, and sad lines bracketed his mouth.

"What's wrong?" I asked.

"I'm sorry I fought so hard against you."

"You loved me." I knew that now. He'd yelled because he was scared, hurt. The same way fear drove my father to drag us from London.

"That doesn't excuse my behavior. It was reprehensible. I was reprehensible. You were right. I didn't act like a man in love. Not when I yelled at you. Not when I abandoned you. Not when I—"

"I'm sorry," I said, lest we be here all day while he outlined his errors.

He froze then blinked twice, as if he still wanted to list his own follies but my apology distracted him. He frowned. "Whatever are you sorry about?"

"For all the times I hurt you. For asking for your help with Mr. Lucas. That's why you left, and I am ashamed of my behavior."

He lifted a dismissive shoulder. "You didn't know."

"But I should have. I—who claimed to know you best—hurt you deeply."

"A fine pair we make." He smiled jaggedly.

"I like to think so."

He chuckled, then cut it off as he caught the undertones of my words. "Do you, truly?"

"I do. Although, if we can learn to disagree without yelling at each other, life would be much sweeter." I threw him a grin.

His face softened with wonder. "I am not dreaming, am I? I've turned that day over and over in my head. What you said, the way you laughed. It was not derisive as I always feared, as your father made it out to be. I know your laughs, each and every one. You laughed with delight, but part of me didn't dare hope."

Yet how he clung to it. My heart melted.

"You had every right to scold me in London. I was a coward and a fool—but no." He shook his head. "Hatfield says I ought not to speak of myself in such defamatory language. Wesley would, but Hatfield thinks it dangerous to consistently belittle oneself."

"Did you just quote a street preacher?"

He gave a sheepish nod. "Hatfield's one of the good ones."

"Mm." I bobbed my eyebrows and bit back a grin. "You were saying?"

"Yes..." Clarence collected himself. "I made many mistakes, and you deserved better. I should like to try and do better if you'll let me."

"I already love you."

A smile swept over him. "How can that sound even sweeter than when I read your declaration?"

"What do you mean read?"

"Your father wrote, confessing his actions and enclosing your letters. I devoured them, reading them so often they are almost in tatters. I'd already made arrangements to come and win you if I could, but those letters were a gift. And yet they pale in comparison to hearing the words from your lips."

Oh! "That's why he said to wait." Seeing Clarence's confusion, I explained, "Father admitted only last week to intercepting my letters, but he didn't mention sending them. When I asked if I could write again, he told me to wait. He must have suspected you'd come. Only, I wish he'd told me. I've been in agony waiting for him to grant me permission."

Clarence laughed, the sound so carefree and reminiscent of our childhood. Then he lunged forward and wrapped me in his arms, pressing my face into his chest. "I should not take such joy in your torment, but it does my heart good to hear how much you love me."

"Shocking behavior, Clarence Beauchamp." I murmured as best I could against his greatcoat.

He pulled back but kept me in the circle of his embrace. A glint burned in his eye. "Do you want to see something truly shocking?"

His head dropped and his lips claimed mine. It was heavenly, better than any dream I'd conjured of this moment when creating princes and dukes in my head. Perhaps, because it was Clarence.

He broke our kiss with a groan. "I promised your father I'd be a gentleman."

"Whyever did you do that?"

A rumble of mirth broke from his chest, and his eyes flashed with a thousand lights. "I promise to kiss you every day after we are wed."

"As long as it is multiple times a day."

"Always, my love. Always."

He took me in his arms again. The steady, rhythmic beat of his heart made my own—the silly, secretive thing—sigh with contentment.

After all these years, we finally understood each other. This blissful euphoria must have been what stirred the Shulamite to say, 'My beloved *is* mine, and I *am* his'. Song of Solomon 2:16 KJV

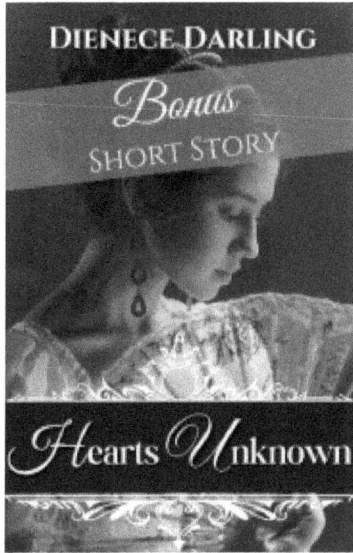

Intrigued by Mr. Hatfield?
Not ready to leave Edith and Clarence?

Sign up to Dienece's newsletter to receive a bonus short story for *Hearts Unknown*, and Hatfield's novelette, *A Heart Unsure*, for free here[1].

Already a subscriber? Use the same link and follow the directions.

---

1. https://dl.bookfunnel.com/ji9erzsk25

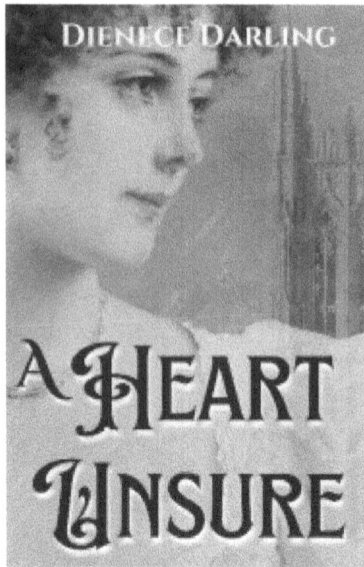

In *A Heart Unsure* an ambitious beauty meets a humble clergyman and has her life turned upside down.

Get A Heart Unsure and the bonus story here[2]!

Author's Note

DEAR READER,

Most of the characters in this book are fictional, but Anne Sizer, George Bell, and John Wesley were real. Anne wandered into a fen and froze to death the bitter winter of 1763. George Bell predicted the world would end on February 28, 1763 and was arrested on the 27th for disturbing the peace. John Wesley wrote twice to the newspapers against Bell and preached in Spitalfields the evening of the 28th. Although, it may have been indoors rather than on the street. A few months later, several of the London society left Wesley's church and followed another man who encouraged dreams and prophecies.

Many reproductions of Wesley's journals skip this difficult part of his history, but I wanted to show that even in our dark moments—when those with envy and strife in their hearts try to undermine God—He can overcome evil with good. His Light can outshine every shade of darkness. Never forget that.

Until Jesus comes, may we be found watching, ready, and faithful. 'Even so, come, Lord Jesus.' Revelation 22:20 KJV

God Bless,

Dienece Darling

Acknowledgments and Permissions

Scriptures used in this book are taken from the King James Version of the Bible.

Rights in the Authorized (King James) Version in the United Kingdom are vested in the Crown. Reproduced by permission of the Crown's patentee, Cambridge University Press.

Cover Design: Dienece Darling

Cover Photography: Cottonbro Studio on https://www.pexels.com.

Edited by Sara R. Turnquist, a true gem

About the Author

Dienece Darling is a former Georgia Belle who calls Australia home these days. She writes inspirational historical fiction and loves to read.

Dienece was a finalist in the First Impressions Contest 2023, the Florida West Coast Writers Competiton 2023, a semi-finalist for the Genesis contest 2022, and a finalist for the CALEB award 2022.

Read more at https://www.dienecedarling.com/.